Barbie in The 12 Dancing PRINCESSES

Adapted by Tennant Redbank

Based on the original screenplay
by Cliff Ruby & Elana Lesser

Random House New York

Princess Genevieve
and her eleven sisters
loved to dance.
They loved to be free.
Some people said
they did not behave.
So their father's cousin
came to help.
Her name was Rowena.

Rowena had a secret.
She wanted to be queen!

She made new rules
for the princesses.
No painting.
No singing.
Above all, no dancing!

The princesses
had new chores.
They had to clean
the garden.
They raked leaves.
It was hard work.

Then the king fell sick.
Rowena nursed him.
She made him tea.

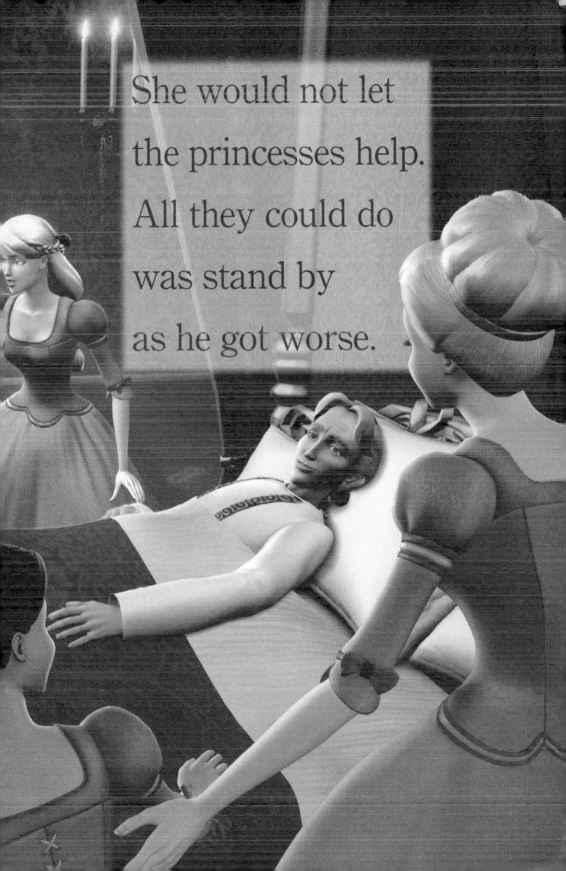

She would not let
the princesses help.
All they could do
was stand by
as he got worse.

The girls were sad.
In their room,
they dreamed
of the magic land
in their favorite book.

Just like in the story,
Genevieve leaped
from stone to stone.
Then she twirled.
The floor opened
to another world!

Gold and silver trees
stood around a lake.
Magic flowers
made wishes come true.
The princesses
danced and danced.
Lacey hurt her knee.
The lake's magic water
healed it right away!

In the morning,
their shoes
were worn out.
Derek, the shoemaker,
gave them new ones.

Genevieve danced
for him.
Step, step, twirl.

Rowena was angry.
She put a guard
outside their door.
She locked them in.
Yet the princesses
danced that night.

On the third night,
the spell would be over.
The girls had to choose
one place or the other.

Their father seemed
better off without them.
They decided to stay
in the magic world.

Derek had found out

Rowena's plan.

He wanted

to tell Genevieve.

He sneaked into

the girls' bedroom.

He saw footprints.

He stepped on them.

He twirled.

The floor opened.

Derek warned the sisters
about Rowena.
They had to go home!
But Rowena had found
the magic world.
She stole two flowers.
Then she trapped
the princesses!
Luckily, they found
another way out.

The king was very sick.

It was from Rowena's tea!

Derek and Genevieve

burst into his room.

Rowena used the dust

from one magic flower.

Two suits of armor

came to life!

They fought Derek.

But he won.

Rowena blew magic dust
at Genevieve.

"Dance your life away!"

Genevieve waved it away.

The dust fell on Rowena.

Her feet began to move.

She could not stop.

She danced
right out of the castle!

Lacey rushed
to her sick father.
She had magic water
from the lake.

She poured a few drops
in his mouth.
It worked!

Soon there was
a royal wedding . . .
for Genevieve and Derek,
princess and shoemaker.
Step, step, twirl.
They were a perfect fit!